This **smelly** book belongs to:

....

PTERODACTYL
(ter-oh-DACT-il)
TRICERATOPS
(tri-SERRA-tops)
BRACHIOSAURUS
(BRAK-ee-oh-sore-us)
IGUANODON
(ig-WHA-noh-don)
BRACHIOSAURUS
(BRAK-ee-oh-sore-us)
PTERODACTYL
(ter-oh-DACT-il)
IGUANODON
(ig-WHA-noh-don)
STEGOSAURUS
(STEG-oh-SORE-us)
PTERODACTYL
(ter-oh-DACT-il)
IGUANODON
(ig-WHA-noh-don)
BRACHIOSAURUS
(BRAK-ee-oh-sore-us)
STEGOSAURUS
(STEG-oh-SORE-us)
TRICERATOPS
(tri-SERRA-tops)

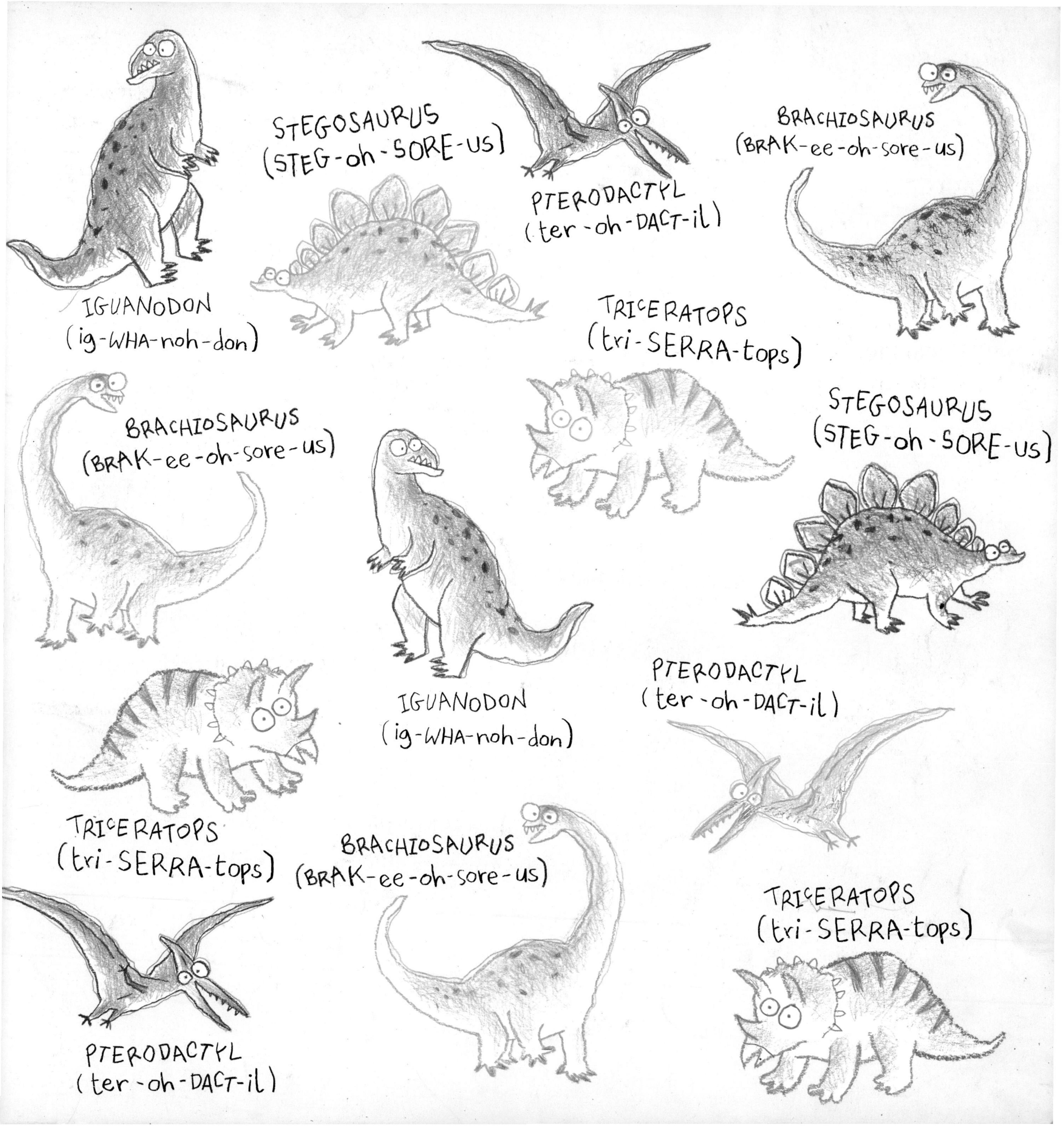
STEGOSAURUS
(STEG-oh-SORE-us)
PTERODACTYL
(ter-oh-DACT-il)
BRACHIOSAURUS
(BRAK-ee-oh-sore-us)
IGUANODON
(ig-WHA-noh-don)
TRICERATOPS
(tri-SERRA-tops)
BRACHIOSAURUS
(BRAK-ee-oh-sore-us)
STEGOSAURUS
(STEG-oh-SORE-us)
IGUANODON
(ig-WHA-noh-don)
PTERODACTYL
(ter-oh-DACT-il)
TRICERATOPS
(tri-SERRA-tops)
BRACHIOSAURUS
(BRAK-ee-oh-sore-us)
TRICERATOPS
(tri-SERRA-tops)
PTERODACTYL
(ter-oh-DACT-il)

To my brother Simon,
we were taught by the best! A.W.

To my friends Jean-François, Rachel,
and Gary their wonderful new baby dinosaur! J.D.

Dinosaur Doo
First published in hardback in 2012
This paperback edition published in 2013

Hodder Children's Books, 338 Euston Road,
London, NW1 3BH
Hodder Children's Books Australia, Level 17/207
Kent Street, Sydney, NSW 2000

A catalogue record of this book is available
from the British Library

ISBN: 978 1 444 90163 4
Printed in China

Hodder Children's Books is a division of
Hachette Children's Books.
An Hachette UK Company.

www.hachette.co.uk

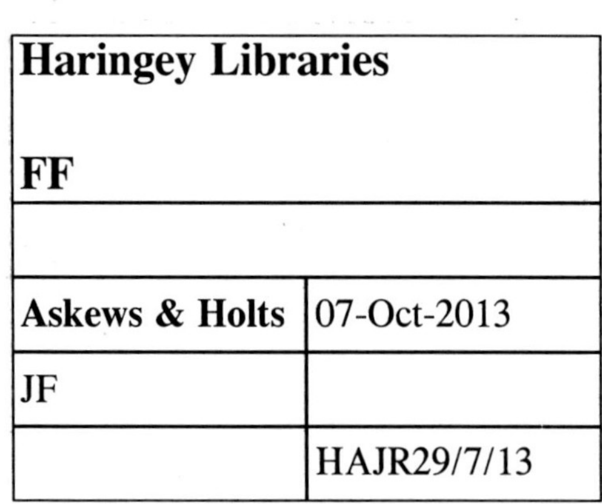

A division of Hachette Children's Books

Andrew Weale & Joelle Dreidemy

Spark lives in a valley that's pretty and green,
He loves to invent: here's his latest machine!
He's trying it out when he suddenly sees
Something that makes him go weak at the knees!

Dinosaurs! Dinosaurs! Up on the hill!

Poor Spark and his friends feel incredibly ill.

For what do the dinosaurs ALL love to do?

Stinky great heap loads of dinosaur POO!

A baby **iguanodon's** first to appear,
It doesn't use nappies or potties! **Oh, dear!**

It's small and it's bouncy. It couldn't be cuter.

But OUT pings its poo! It's a mini pea-shooter!

A strong **stegosaurus** lifts its tail high,

And shoots like a cannon, right up to the sky!

Then Spark and his friends
hear a plippety plopping,

Oh no! It's a stinky **triceratops** dropping!

Everyone hears a loud ROAR and they see
A brachiosaurus, tall as a tree!

It wiggles its botty, it's such a sweet pet,
Then gives them a shower that they'll never forget!

Soon everyone’s swimming in torrents of poo,
They’re up to their ears in this dinosaur doo!

Then Spark cries:
EUREKA!
'I've got an idea.
I know how to make all this
poo disappear!'

Spark tells all his friends to dig a huge hole,

And roll down some boulders and make a big bowl!

They dig a deep channel and fill it with pipes,

And make a great roll of deluxe botty wipes!

They cut down a tree,
they saw and they chop,
And make a round seat
with a lid on the top.

They join lots of hoops
and then make a long chain,

And lift it up high with an old-fashioned crane.

The very next day as the sun starts to rise,

Spark gives all the dinosaurs quite a surprise!

'When you want to go for a dinosaur poo,

You **MUST** use this poo-tiful dinosaur loo!'

The dinosaurs really adore their new loo,

They ALL want to use it, just look at that queue!

They flush when they're done, they're extremely polite,

And washing their paws is a dino delight.

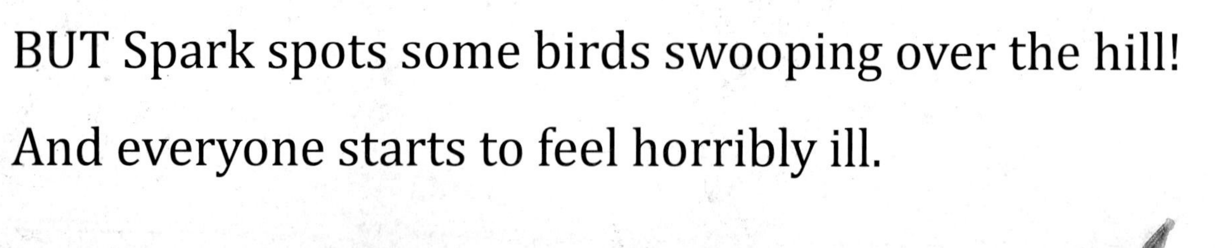

BUT Spark spots some birds swooping over the hill!

And everyone starts to feel horribly ill.

For what do the birds love to do when they swoop?

Dinosaur birds love to dinosaur

PTERODACTYL
(ter-oh-DACT-il)
TRICERATOPS
(tri-SERRA-tops)
BRACHIOSAURUS
(BRAK-ee-oh-sore-us)
IGUANODON
(ig-WHA-noh-don)
BRACHIOSAURUS
(BRAK-ee-oh-sore-us)
PTERODACTYL
(ter-oh-DACT-il)
IGUANODON
(ig-WHA-noh-don)
STEGOSAURUS
(STEG-oh-SORE-us)
PTERODACTYL
(ter-oh-DACT-il)
IGUANODON
(ig-WHA-noh-don)
BRACHIOSAURUS
(BRAK-ee-oh-sore-us)
STEGOSAURUS
(STEG-oh-SORE-us)
TRICERATOPS
(tri-SERRA-tops)

IGUANODON
(ig-WHA-noh-don)

STEGOSAURUS
(STEG-oh-SORE-us)

PTERODACTYL
(ter-oh-DACT-il)
BRACHIOSAURUS
(BRAK-ee-oh-sore-us)

TRICERATOPS
(tri-SERRA-tops)

BRACHIOSAURUS
(BRAK-ee-oh-sore-us)

IGUANODON
(ig-WHA-noh-don)

STEGOSAURUS
(STEG-oh-SORE-us)

PTERODACTYL
(ter-oh-DACT-il)

TRICERATOPS
(tri-SERRA-tops)

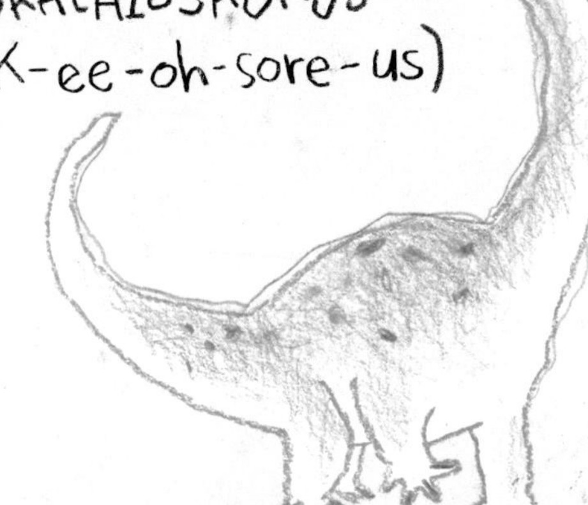
BRACHIOSAURUS
(BRAK-ee-oh-sore-us)

PTERODACTYL
(ter-oh-DACT-il)

TRICERATOPS
(tri-SERRA-tops)

Other fabulous
Hodder books
DAVE
Written by
Sue
Hendra
Illustrated by
Liz Pichon
"I laughed so much I farted!"
Edward, aged 6
9781 444 91295 1
I Really Want to Eat a Child
Sylviane Donnio • Dorothée de Monfreid
9780 340 97049 2
A COUNTING BOOK
ONE NEWT IN A SUIT
ANDREW WEALE
AND
MARGARET CHAMBERLAIN
9780 340 98868 8
THE VERY CRANKY BEAR
NICK BLAND
9780 340 98943 2
ALEX T. SMITH
CATCH US IF YOU CAN-CAN
9781 444 90366 9
The Big Animal Mix-Up
GUESS WHO'S UNDER THE FLAPS!
Gareth Edwards
Kanako Usui
9780 340 98989 0